DOGGER'S CHRISTMAS

For Ed, Tom and Clara,
with very much love

RED FOX

UK | USA | Canada | Ireland | Australia | India | New Zealand | South Africa

Red Fox is part of the Penguin Random House group of companies
whose addresses can be found at global.penguinrandomhouse.com.

www.penguin.co.uk   www.puffin.co.uk   www.ladybird.co.uk

Penguin
Random House
UK

First published in hardback by The Bodley Head 2020
This paperback edition published 2021

001

Printed in China

The authorized representative in the EEA is Penguin Random House Ireland,
Morrison Chambers, 32 Nassau Street, Dublin D02 YH68

A CIP catalogue record for this book is available from the British Library

ISBN: 978–1–782–95977–9

All correspondence to:
Red Fox
Penguin Random House Children's
One Embassy Gardens, 8 Viaduct Gardens, London SW11 7BW

DOGGER'S
CHRISTMAS

Shirley Hughes

RED FOX

Once there was a boy called Dave. He had a big sister called Bella and a little brother called Joe.

Joe could not walk properly yet, but he could scrabble along on the floor, crawling very fast.

Bella was specially good at running and jumping. She could turn cartwheels and stand on her head.

Dave had a very favourite toy called Dogger, who was almost as old as he was. He still took him to bed with him every night.

But now he was getting interested in all sorts
of other toys, like his train set . . .

and his spaceship, and cars that you could wind up
so that they would whizz about very fast on their own.

Christmas was coming soon. Dave and Bella helped Mum and
Dad to put up the paper chains and decorate the tree.

They knew all about it being the birthday of baby Jesus and
how he did not have a proper bed and had to sleep in a manger,
and was visited by angels and shepherds and wise men.

Dave and Bella were very busy
making lists of all the fancy stuff
they were hoping to get as
presents, and posting them up
the chimney to Father Christmas.

Bella did not want any more teddies because she had
seven already. She was asking for some new trainers
and a T-shirt with an Olympic badge on it,
and a really good skipping rope because
the one she had was rather babyish.

Dave wanted lots more track for his
train set and some building bricks,
a book about wild animals and a
chocolate reindeer. Mum helped
him make his list.

Mum took Dave and Bella Christmas shopping. Joe was too young for that, so he stayed at home with Dad. They did not take Dogger either, in case he got lost.

Dave left Dogger propped up on the windowsill,
waiting for them to come back.

They were gone a very long time.

On Christmas Eve the tree was all alight in the front
window, and Dave and Bella had their Christmas stockings
ready to hang up.

Dave had meant to give Dogger a stocking too, but there
was so much excitement going on that he forgot.

When at last they were cuddled down together Dave found it very hard to get to sleep. He knew that Father Christmas would not come until he was asleep, but somehow he kept sitting up and checking the end of the bed to make quite sure that his stocking was easy to see.

But in the end all the house was quiet.

At last it was Christmas morning and Dave, Bella and
Joe woke up very early to find their stockings full of
all sorts of lovely presents. The floor around their beds
was covered with torn wrapping paper.

As soon as Mum and Dad were awake Dave and Bella gave them their presents, which they had kept secretly hidden.

Dave had some lovely sweet-smelling soap for Mum, which Dad had helped him choose.

And a bag of chocolate coins for Dad.

Bella had a little diary for Dad which he could take into his office and a book about wildflowers for Mum.

After breakfast Mum and
Bella went over to see Jim Baker
who lived on his own with
his dog Ruffy. Mum had
a box of chocolates
for him, and Bella
had made him a card.
She also had a tin
of dog food for Ruffy
who was her
special friend.

"My son Phil's coming
over to see me and
bringing the Christmas
dinner," Jim said.
"Bound to be late –
but it will be great to
see him when he does
turn up."

Meanwhile
Dave and Joe
had stayed at
home with Dad
who was keeping
an eye on the
Christmas dinner.
Dave started to
build a super space
station with his new
building bricks.

Then Granny and Grandpa arrived, bringing presents, and Christmas had really begun.

It was a lovely day.

At bedtime that night, when Grandma and Grandpa had left, the children were very tired and very happy. Joe was tucked up and Dave was already fast asleep when Dad carried him upstairs to bed. Bella followed very soon after.

Later that evening when Dad was cleaning up the Christmas wrapping paper and putting it into a big plastic bag,

and Mum was filling the dishwasher, they heard a wail. Dave had woken up and wanted Dogger.

But where was he?

They looked everywhere,
but he was nowhere to
be found.

Dave cried and cried. He felt so sad that Dogger,
his dear old friend, had been forgotten and left out
of all the Christmas fun. It took him a long time
to get to sleep . . .

In the following days Dave did not want to play with his new toys. Christmas was no good without Dogger. Mum reminded him that Dogger had been lost before and had turned up in the end. He was sure to be in the house somewhere.

But Dave was not reassured. His misery spread through the whole family. No matter how hard they all searched, Dogger seemed to have disappeared. Dave began to think that this time he might be lost forever.

Dad was doing a lot of clearing-up. Dave and Bella
stood in the doorway and watched sadly as he tied
up the Christmas rubbish bag and took it out to the
place where they kept the bins.

The refuse van was already making its way noisily up the street and the bin men were emptying the brimming bins into the back of it, so that all the contents were scrunched up inside.

They were nearly at Dave and Bella's house when, suddenly, Bella had a very clever idea. She decided to have one last look for Dogger! Bella dashed over to the bin, emptied the rubbish out all over the path and began searching through it.

And guess what?

Out of a big piece of screwed-up
wrapping paper she caught
sight of the tip of a little
brown tail.

"Dogger!" she shouted.
"Dogger!" shouted Dave.
Bella pulled him out and held him up high.
He was very dirty. Dave was so pleased.
He gave out a cry of joy, ran down to the
front gate, took Dogger from her hands
and hugged him tight.

"We thought he was lost!" Bella told the bin men.
And they all raised a cheer.

Then, of course, Dave and Bella helped Dad to clear up
every bit of rubbish which had been tipped out and get it
back into the bin.

"Phew! That was a near thing!" said Dad later, when they were all sitting among the presents.

Dave was tenderly wiping some
dust from Dogger with a piece of
tissue paper.

   He was too happy
to speak. He had
Dogger back and
that was all that
mattered.

Happy Christmas, Dogger!